She liked being quiet.
It meant she noticed all
the small things in
the forest,

and could make up wonderful
stories about them. The only
problem was . . .

. . . all her friends were really, really **noisy**!

Whenever Fox tried to tell them
one of her stories, they were far
too noisy to hear.

One day, they were all playing pirates.

"Ahoy, me hearties!" hooted Owl.

"Shiver me timbers!" shouted Squirrel.

They were the **noisiest** they'd ever been. Suddenly Raccoon noticed how sad Fox was. "Avast, ye! STOP!" he shouted.

And they did.

Fox explained why she was sad.
"I really want to tell you a story, but you're
always being too noisy!"

Her friends were very sorry.
"We love stories!" they said. "Tell us one now!"

They gathered round, and Fox began: "Once upon a time there was a bear . . ."

"A bear?" shouted Squirrel. "I know! Let's **all** pretend to be bears!"

"Wait!"
said Fox, as the
others ran off,
roaring.

"I haven't finished
my story!"

But her noisy friends
had already dashed up a tree.

"We're climbing!" they shouted.
"Just like bears! Come on, Fox!
Come and be a bear!"

But quiet little Fox
had noticed something: some
absolutely enormous claw marks!

"Shhh!" she said. "I think there
might be a **real** bear."

But her noisy friends had
already jumped into the river.

"We're splashing!"
they shouted. "Just like bears!
Come and splash, too, Fox!"
But quiet little Fox had noticed
something else: some absolutely
enormous paw prints!

"Shhh!" she whispered.
"I'm sure there's a bear!"

But her noisy friends were already scampering over a bridge.

"We're **roaring!**" they shouted. "Just like bears! Raaaaagh!"

But quiet little Fox had heard something worrying: a big, deep, rumbly, grouchy

G-R-O-W-L!!!

"Shhhh! Quiet!" she said. "I really think there's a bear!"

"Of course there's a bear!" shouted Squirrel.

"We're all bears!"

And they carried on roaring.

Fox felt the ground shiver and shake. It was definitely a bear!
She had to warn her friends – but how could she make them listen?
She'd have to shout, louder than she'd ever shouted before . . .

BE QUIET!!!

Everyone heard her that time!
They all stopped shouting.

Then Squirrel said:
"I don't like being quiet."
"But there's a bear!"
whispered Fox.

"Where?" shouted her friends.

RAAARGH!!!

roared the absolutely
enormous real bear.

"Quick! Hide!" said Fox. She pushed and tumbled
and squeezed them inside an old tree trunk.

"Help!" shouted Squirrel.
"I'm scared!" yelled Raccoon.
"HOOOOOT!" hooted Owl, who was
too frightened to say anything else.

"Shhhhh!" said Fox. "Listen!"

There was a strange noise outside.
It sounded like someone crying.

Fox bravely peeped out. To her surprise,
she saw tears rolling down the bear's nose.

They all tiptoed up to him.

"You were so noisy, you woke me up,"
cried the bear, "and now I can't
get back to sleep!"

"Sorry," said Squirrel.
"We were being bears."

Then Owl had an idea: "Maybe Fox
could tell you a bedtime story?
She tells really good stories."

"Oh, yes!" said Raccoon.
"Tell us the story of how you
found the bear!"

So Fox began:
"Once upon a time, there
was a fox who was very, very quiet.
Because she was quiet, she noticed all
the small things in the forest. And that's
how she spotted the claw marks and
paw marks of a great big
sleepy bear!"

As Fox told her story,
everyone listened
very quietly.

They laughed at the
funny bits.

They shivered at
the scary bits.

"And then," said Fox, "when the story was over, all the friends yawned . . .

and stretched . . .

and they all fell fast asleep . . .

"... just like bears!"

For Felix

First published in the UK in 2020 by Alison Green Books
An imprint of Scholastic Children's Books
Euston House, 24 Eversholt Street, London NW1 1DB

A division of Scholastic Ltd
www.scholastic.co.uk

London – New York – Toronto – Sydney – Auckland
Mexico City – New Delhi – Hong Kong

Designed by Zoë Tucker
Text and illustrations copyright © 2020 Nicola Kinnear

HB ISBN: 978 1 407188 85 0
PB ISBN: 978 1 407188 86 7

All rights reserved.
Printed in Malaysia

1 3 5 7 9 10 8 6 4 2

The moral rights of Nicola Kinnear have been asserted.

Papers used by Scholastic Children's Books are made
from wood grown in sustainable forests.